Usborne English Readers

Starter Level

The Sun and the Wind

Retold by Laura Cowan

Illustrated by Jessica Knight

English language consultant: Peter Viney

Contents

You can listen to the story online here:
www.usborneenglishreaders.com/
sunandthewind

The Sun lives in the sky. He shines all day. The Wind is his friend in the sky.

The Sun and the Wind look down on the world, and they talk about the people there.

Sometimes they play games. The Wind likes games. He likes songs too, and he sings very well. But today, the Wind isn't happy.

"What's the matter?" asks the Sun. "Don't you like it up here?"

"No, it's boring," the Wind answers. He flies sadly around the sky.

"Do you want to sing?" the Sun asks. "I can't sing very well, but I can try."

"No, not today," the Wind answers.

"Do you want to play a game, then?" the Sun asks.

"No," says the Wind. "Games are boring, too."

"Really?" says the Sun. "You love games."

"All right, but I want to play my new game," says the Wind.

"Do I know it? Is it an easy game?" asks the Sun. "Well, it's easy for *me*," says the Wind.

I like my new game.

"Can you see that girl down there?" asks the Wind. "She's wearing a red coat."

The Sun looks down. Only
one person is wearing a red coat.
She's walking slowly.

Yes, I can
see her.

"Well," says the Wind, "Can you
take her coat off? That's the game."
The Sun laughs. "All right, let's
play," he says. "Can I start?"

"No, *I* want to start!" shouts
the Wind. He flies down to the girl.
He blows and he blows, but he can't
blow the girl's coat off.

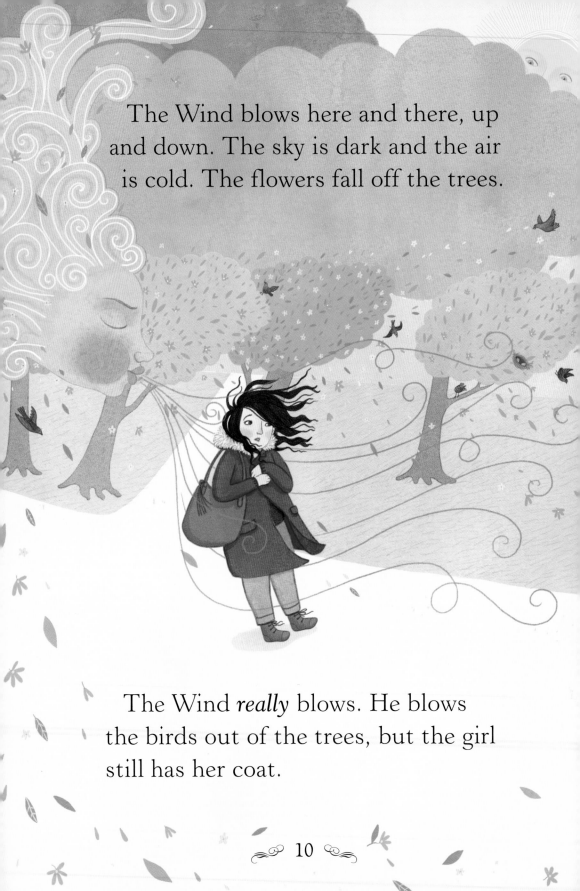

The Wind blows here and there, up and down. The sky is dark and the air is cold. The flowers fall off the trees.

The Wind *really* blows. He blows the birds out of the trees, but the girl still has her coat.

The girl walks quickly "Oh, it's cold! Where is the Sun?"

"This isn't working!" The Wind is angry. "I don't understand."

Can I try now?

"All right, you try,"
says the Wind.
The Sun smiles again.
Then he shines brightly. The
birds sing in the trees. The sky is blue.
Doors open, and children run out
of their houses.

The Sun shines and shines. The girl stops and smiles. "That's better. It's nice and warm," she says.

"What is she doing?" shouts the Wind. "Is she taking her coat off now?"

The Sun just smiles and shines.
"What a beautiful day!" says the girl.
She is happy.

The Sun is smiling, but the Wind
doesn't speak. He's angry.

"So, do I win?" the Sun asks. He waits. Slowly, the Wind says, "Yes, you win... but why?"

"When you blow, people are cold and sad. When I shine, they are warm and happy. I am kind to the girl and she likes me," the Sun says.

"It's always good to be kind."

Weather words

Sun and wind are words we use to talk about the weather. Here are some more weather words:

Rain

Cloud

Snow

Storm

Do you have snow in your town or in your country?
What kind of weather do you like best?

Activities

The answers are on page 24.

Can you see all these things in the picture?
Which three things *can't* you see?

sea   house   tree   child

chair   town   coat   clock

door   bird   table   dog

Talk about people in the story

Choose the right words.

happy	kind	clean
funny	quick	cold

1.

The Wind isn't ....

2.

The girl is ....

3.

The Sun is ....

What's happening?

Which three sentences go with picture 1?
Which go with picture 2?

1.

A. The girl is cold.

B. The girl is happy.

C. The sky is blue.

2.

D. The girl is
    wearing her coat.

E. The girl is warm.

F. The sky is dark.

What are they thinking?

Choose the right sentence for each picture.

It's always good to be kind.

What is the Wind's new game?

I want to take the girl's coat off.

1.

2.

3.

What is the Wind saying?

There are some wrong words here.
Can you choose the right word?

1.

Every house is the same.

coat   day   story

2.

Dogs are boring.

Cats   Songs   People

3.

I like my new coat.

game   book   house

Word list

around (prep) a word that explains where something is or how it is moving.

blow (v) to push air from your mouth. The wind blows, too.

boring (adj) not fun or interesting.

brightly (adv) giving lots of light.

kind (adj) Kind people are nice to other people and want to help them.

shine (v) to give light. The sun shines. The moon and stars shine, too.

sky

sun
shining

shout (v) to say something very loudly. Sometimes people shout when they are angry.

sky (n) The sky is above us. On a sunny day, the sky is blue.

still (adv) when something is still happening, it doesn't change. For example, "9A.M.: it's raining. 10A.M.: it's still raining."

warm (adj) not cold, hot in a nice way.

win (v) when you win a game or a race, you are first or you do best.

wind (n) air moving quickly.

wind blowing

Answers

Can you see all these things in the picture?

Three things you can't see:
chair, clock, table.

Talk about people in the story

1. happy
2. cold
3. kind

What's happening?

1 - A, D, F.
2 - B, C, E.

What are they thinking?

1. What is the Wind's new game?
2. I want to take the girl's coat off.
3. It's always good to be kind.

What is the Wind saying?

1. ~~house~~ day
2. ~~Dogs~~ Songs
3. ~~coat~~ game

You can find information about other Usborne English Readers here:
www.usborneenglishreaders.com

Designed by Sam Whibley
Series designer: Laura Nelson Norris
Edited by Mairi Mackinnon

First published in 2019 by Usborne Publishing Ltd.,
Usborne House, 83-85 Saffron Hill, London EC1N 8RT, England.
www.usborne.com Copyright © 2019 Usborne Publishing Ltd.